A Cuddle for Claude

David Wojtowycz

GULLANE
CHILDREN'S BOOKS

Claude woke up from his afternoon nap. In his dream
he had been cuddling his blanket, but what he really
wanted was a proper cuddle from his Mum.

So he went to find her.

Mum had her hands full of groceries.
"Hello Claude," she said, "Are you up already?"
She kissed him on the forehead. "I'll give
you a great big cuddle, Claude, but I
just have a few things to finish first.
Why don't you read your books
and I'll come as soon as I can."

Claude went to the bookshelf and took out his favourite book. He read and read - at least *four* pages.

Then he went to find Mum. She was mixing some sticky stuff in a bowl. "Have you finished reading already?" she said, glancing at the clock. "I'd give you a cuddle, Claude, but my hands are all covered with flour. Why don't you draw a picture and I'll come and cuddle you just as soon as I can."

Claude sat at his desk. He drew and drew until there was no paper left.

Then he went to find Mum.
  "Have you finished your picture
already?" she asked, as she
took her baking out of the oven.
"I'd give you a cuddle, Claude, but
this tray is very hot. Why don't you
do your puzzle and I'll come and
cuddle you just as soon as I can."

Claude pulled out his best
jigsaw puzzle. He put all
the pieces together.
They didn't look quite
right, but he was
sure Mum *must*
be ready by now.

But she wasn't.
  "Have you finished your puzzle already?"
Mum said, when Claude appeared.

"I must just finish this, Claude, then I *promise* I'll come and cuddle you."

Claude was fed up. He'd read *four* pages
of his book, drawn *loads* of pictures, and done
his most difficult jigsaw puzzle – well nearly.
But Mum still hadn't given him his cuddle.

how tall am I?

There could only
be one explanation:
she didn't love him anymore!
He packed his toys into his blanket.

Mum finished at last.
She called to Claude, but he was
nowhere to be seen.

Then she spotted a trail of toys leading into the garden.

Claude was sitting on his
blanket under the big tree.
"What are you doing out
here?" asked Mum.
Claude looked very sad.
"Oh, Claude!" said Mum and
she took him by the hand.

"I'm sorry I was too busy to cuddle you," said Mum, "I just wanted everything to be ready for your surprise."

Mum showed Claude the table. It was laid out with a delicious tea, including Claude's favourite freshly-baked cookies. Just then the doorbell rang.

"Surprise!" laughed the 'surprise',
as she popped her head around
the door.
It was Grandma!

"Now can *I* have a cuddle?" asked Mum.
 "Me too!" laughed Grandma. And they all gave each other the biggest

Cuddle

they could!

for my Mum XXX